The Shooting
of
Dan McGrew

and other poems

dog pic

Robert W. Service

Art Work by Mariken Van Nimwegen

hancock

house

ISBN 0-88839-224-9
Copyright © 1989 Hancock House

Canadian Cataloguing in Publication Data

Service, Robert W., 1874 - 1958
    The shooting of Dan McGrew

ISBN 0-88839-224-9
I. Title.

PS8537.E78S56 1989   C811'.52   C89-091219-X
PR9199.3.S45S56   1989

Printed in Hong Kong

Published simultaneously in Canada and the United States by

HANCOCK HOUSE PUBLISHERS LTD.
19313 Zero Ave., Surrey, B.C. V3S 5J9

HANCOCK HOUSE PUBLISHERS
1431 Harrison Ave., Blaine, WA 98230

Table of Contents

The Men that Don't Fit In

There's a race of men that don't fit in,
    A race that can't stay still;
So they break the hearts of kith and kin,
    And they roam the world at will.
They range the field and they rove the flood,
    And they climb the mountain's crest.
Theirs is the curse of the gypsy blood,
    And they don't know how to rest.

If they just went straight, they might go far;
    They are strong and brave and true;
But they're always tired of the things that are,
    And they want the strange and new.
They say: "Could I find my proper groove,
    What a deep mark I would make!"
So they chop and change, and each fresh move
    Is only a fresh mistake.

And each forgets, as he strips and runs
    With a brilliant, fitful pace,
It's the steady quiet, plodding ones
    Who win in the lifelong race.
And each forgets that his youth has fled,
    Forgets that his prime is past,

Till he stands one day with a hope that's dead,
    In the glare of the truth at last.

He has failed, he has failed;
      he has missed his chance;
    He has just done things by half.
Life's been a jolly good joke on him,
    And now is the time to laugh.
Ha, ha! He is one of the Legion Lost;
    He was never meant to win.
He's a rolling stone, and it's bred in the bone;
    He's a man who won't fit in.

The Trail of 'Ninety-Eight

Gold! We leapt from our benches.
    Gold! We sprang from our stools.
  Gold! We wheeled in the furrow,
    fired with the faith of fools.
Fearless, unfound, unfitted,
    far from the night and the cold,
Heard we the clarion summons,
    followed the master-lure—Gold

Men from the sands of the Sunland;
    men from the woods of the West;
Men from the farms and the cities,
    into the Northland we pressed.
Graybeards and striplings and women,
    good men and bad men and bold,
Leaving our homes and our loved ones,
    crying exultantly, "Gold!"

Never was seen such an army,
    pitiful, futile, unfit;
Never was seen such a spirit,
    manifold courage and grit.
Never has been such a cohort
    under one banner unrolled

As surged to the ragged-edged Arctic,
    urged by the arch-tempter—Gold.

"Farewell!" we cried to our dearests;
    little we cared for their tears.
  "Farewell!" we cried to the humdrum
    and the yoke of the hireling years;
Just like a pack of school-boys,
  and the big crowd cheered us good-bye.
Never were hearts so uplifted,
    never were hopes so high.

The spectral shores flitted past us,
    and every whirl of the screw
Hurled us nearer to fortune,
    and ever we planned what we'd do—
Do with the gold when we got it—
    big, shiny nuggets like plums,
There in the sand of the river,
    gouging it out with our thumbs.

And one man wanted a castle,
    another a racing stud;
A third would cruise in a palace yacht
    like a red-necked prince of blood.
And so we dreamed and we vaunted,
    millionaires to a man,
Leaping to wealth in our visions
    long ere the trail began.

II.

We landed in wind-swept Skagway.

We joined the weltering mass,

Clamoring over their outfits,

waiting to climb the Pass.

We tightened our girths and our pack-straps;

we linked on the Human Chain,

Struggling up to the summit,
    where every step was a pain.

Gone was the joy of our faces,
    grim and haggard and pale;
    The heedless mirth of the shipboard
    was changed to the care of the trail.
We flung ourselves in the struggle,
    packing our grub in relays,
    Step by step to the summit
    in the bale of the winter days.

Floundering deep in the sump-holes,
    stumbling out again;
    Crying with cold and weakness,
    crazy with fear and pain.
Then from the depths of our travail,
    ere our spirits were broke,
    Grim, tenacious and savage,
    the lust of the trail awoke.

For grub meant gold to our thinking,
      and all that could walk must pack;
    The sheep for the shambles stumbled,
      each with a load on its back;
And even the swine were burdened,
      and grunted and squealed and rolled,
    And men went mad in the moment,
      huskily clamoring, "Gold!"

"Klondike or bust!" rang the slogan;
      every man for his own.
    Oh, how we flogged the horses,
      staggering skin and bone!
Oh, how we cursed their weakness,
      anguish they could not tell,
    Breaking their hearts in our passion,
      lashing them on till they fell!

Oh, we were brutes and devils,
      goaded by lust and fear!
    Our eyes were strained to the summit;
      the weakling dropped to the rear,
Falling in heaps by the trail-side,
      heart-broken, limp, and wan;
    But the gaps closed up in an instant,
      and heedless the chain went on.

Never will I forget it,
      there on the mountain face,
    Antlike, men with their burdens,
      clinging in icy space;
Dogged, determined and dauntless,
      cruel and callous and cold,

Cursing, blaspheming, reviling,
    and ever that battle-cry—"Gold!"

Thus toiled we, the army of fortune,
    in hunger and hope and despair,
Till glacier, mountain and forest
    vanished, and, radiantly fair,
There at our feet lay Lake Bennett,
    and down to its welcome we ran:
The trail of the land was over,
    the trail of the water began.

III.

We built our boats and we launched them.
    Never has been such a fleet;
A packing-case for a bottom,
    a mackinaw for a sheet.
Shapeless, grotesque, lopsided,
    flimsy, makeshift and crude,
Each man after his fashion
    builded as best he could.

Each man worked like a demon,
    as prow to rudder we raced;
The winds of the Wild cried "Hurry!"
    the voice of the waters, "Haste!"
We hated those driving before us;
    we dreaded those pressing behind;
We cursed the slow current that bore us;
    we prayed to the God of the wind.

Spring! and the hillsides flourished,
    vivid in jewelled green;

Spring! and our hearts' blood nourished
    envy and hatred and spleen.
Little cared we for the Spring-birth;
    much cared we to get on—
Stake in the Great White Channel,
    stake ere the best be gone.

The greed of the gold possessed us;
    pity and love were forgot;
Covetous visions obsessed us;
    brother with brother fought.
Partner with partner wrangled,
    each one claiming his due;

Wrangled and halved their outfits,
    sawing their boats in two.

Thuswise we voyaged Lake Bennett,
    Tagish, then Windy Arm,
Sinister, savage and baleful,
    boding us hate and harm.
Many a scow was shattered
    there on that iron shore;
Many a heart was broken
    straining at sweep and oar.

We roused Lake Marsh with a chorus,
    we drifted many a mile.
There was the canyon before us—
    cave-like its dark defile;
The shores swept faster and faster;
    the river narrowed to wrath;
Waters that hissed disaster
    reared upright in our path.

Beneath us the green tumult churning,
    above us the cavernous gloom;
Around us, swift twisting and turning,
    the black, sullen walls of a tomb.
We spun like a chip in a mill-race;
    our hearts hammered under the test;
Then—oh, the relief on each chill face!—
    we soared into sunlight and rest.

Hand sought for hand on the instant.
    Cried we, "Our troubles are o'er!"
Then, like a rumble of thunder,

heard we a canorous roar.
Leaping and boiling and seething,
    saw we a cauldron afume;
  There was the rage of the rapids,
    there was the menace of doom.

The river springs like a racer,
    sweeps through a gash in the rock;
Butts at the boulder-ribbed bottom,
    staggers and rears at the shock;
Leaps like a terrified monster,
    writhes in its fury and pain;
Then with the crash of a demon
    springs to the onset again.

Dared we that ravening terror;
    heard we its din in our ears;
Called on the Gods of our fathers,
    juggled forlorn with our fears;
Sank to our waists in its fury,
    tossed to the sky like a fleece;
Then, when our dread was the greatest,
    crashed into safety and peace.

But what of the others that followed,
    losing their boats by the score?
Well could we see them and hear them,
    strung down that desolate shore.
What of the poor souls that perished?
    Little of them shall be said—
On to the Golden Valley!
    Pause not to bury the dead.

Then there were days of drifting,
  breezes soft as a sigh;
  Night trailed her robe of jewels
   over the floor of the sky.
The moonlit stream was a python,
  silver, sinuous, vast,
  That writhed on a shroud of velvet—
   well, it was done at last.

There were the tents of Dawson,
  there the scar of the slide;
  Swiftly we poled o'er the shallows,
   swiftly leapt o'er the side.
Fires fringed the mouth of Bonanza;
  sunset gilded the dome;
  The test of the trail was over—
   thank God, thank God, we were Home!

The Shooting of Dan McGrew

A bunch of the boys were whooping it up
    in the Malamute saloon;
  The kid that handles the music-box
    was hitting a jag-time tune;
Back of the bar, in a solo game,
    sat Dangerous Dan McGrew,
  And watching his luck was his light-o'-love,
    the lady that's known as Lou.

When out of the night, which was fifty below,
    and into the din and the glare,
  There stumbled a miner fresh from the creeks,
    dog-dirty, and loaded for bear.
He looked like a man with a foot in the grave
    and scarcely the strength of a louse,
  Yet he tilted a poke of dust on the bar,
    and he called for drinks for the house.
There was none could place the stranger's face,
    though we searched ourselves for a clue;
  But we drank his health, and the last to drink
    was Dangerous Dan McGrew.

There's men that somehow just grip your eyes,
    and hold them hard like a spell;

And such was he, and he looked to me
    like a man who had lived in hell;
With a face most hair, and the dreary stare
    of a dog whose day is done,
As he watered the green stuff in his glass,
    and the drops fell one by one.
Then I got to figgering who he was,
    and wondering what he'd do,
And I turned my head—and there watching him
    was the lady that's known as Lou.

His eyes went rubbering round the room,
    and he seemed in a kind of daze,
Till at last that old piano fell
    in the way of his wandering gaze.
The ragtime kid was having a drink;
    there was no one else on the stool,
So the stranger stumbles across the room,
    and flops down there like a fool.
In a buckskin shirt that was glazed with dirt
    he sat, and I saw him sway;

Then he clutched the keys with his talon hands
  —my God, but that man could play!

Were you ever out in the Great Alone,
    when the moon was awful clear,
And the icy mountains hemmed you in
    with a silence you most could *hear;*
With only the howl of a timber wolf,
    and you camped there in the cold,
A half-dead thing in a stark, dead world,
    clean mad for the muck called gold;
While high overhead, green, yellow and red,
    the North Lights swept in bars?—
Then you've a hunch what the music meant...
    hunger and night and the stars.

And hunger not of the belly kind
    that's banished with bacon and beans,
But the gnawing hunger of lonely men
    for a home and all that it means;
For a fireside far from the cares that are,
    four walls and a roof above;
But oh! so cramful of cozy joy,
    and crowned with a woman's love—
A woman dearer than all the world,
    and true as Heaven is true...
    (God! how ghastly she looks through her rouge—
    the lady that's known as Lou.)

Then on a sudden the music changed,
    so soft that you scarce could hear;
But you felt that your life had been looted clean
    of all that it once held dear;

That someone had stolen the woman you loved;
    that her love was a devil's lie;
That your guts were gone, and the best for you
    was to crawl away and die.
'Twas the crowning cry of a heart's despair,
    and it thrilled you through and through—
"I guess I'll make it a spread misere,"
    said Dangerous Dan McGrew.

The music almost died away...
    then it burst like a pent-up flood;
And it seemed to say, "Repay, repay,"
    and my eyes were blind with blood.
The thought came back of an ancient wrong,
    and it stung like a frozen lash,
And the lust awoke to kill, to kill...
    then the music stopped with a crash,
And the stranger turned, and his eyes they burned
    in a most peculiar way;

In a buckskin shirt that was glazed with dirt
     he sat, and I saw him sway;
Then his lips went in in a kind of grin,
     and he spoke, and his voice was calm,
  And "Boys," says he, "you don't know me,
     and none of you care a damn;
But I want to state, and my words are straight,
     and I'll bet my poke they're true,
That one of you is a hound of hell...
     and that one is Dan McGrew."

Then I ducked my head, and the lights went out,
     and two guns blazed in the dark,
And a woman screamed, and the lights went up,
     and two men lay stiff and stark.
Pitched on his head, and pumped full of lead,
     was Dangerous Dan McGrew,
  While the man from the creeks lay clutched to the breast
     of the lady that's known as Lou.

These are the simple facts of the case,
     and I guess I ought to know.
  They say that the stranger was crazed with "hooch,"
     and I'm not denying it's so.
I'm not so wise as the lawyer guys,
     but strictly between us two—
  The woman that kissed him—and pinched his poke—
     was the lady that's known as Lou.

The Ballad of Gum-Boot Ben

He was an old prospector with a vision bleared and dim.
He asked me for a grubstake, and the same I gave to him.
He hinted of a hidden trove, and when I made so bold
To question his veracity, this is the tale he told:

"I do not seek the copper streak,
        nor yet the yellow dust;
    I am not fain for sake of gain
        to irk the frozen crust;
Let fellows gross find gilded dross,
        far other is my mark;
    Oh, gentle youth, this is the truth—
        I go to seek the Ark.

"I prospected the Pelly bed,
        I prospected the White;
    The Nordenscold for love of gold
        I piked from morn till night;
Afar and near for many a year
        I led the wild stampede,
    Until I guessed that all my quest
        was vanity and greed.

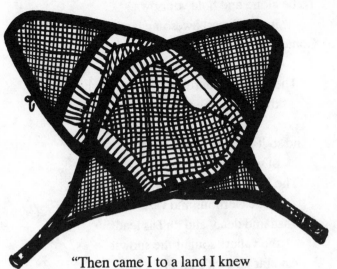

"Then came I to a land I knew
  no man had ever seen,
A haggard land, forlornly spanned
  by mountains lank and lean;
The nitchies said 'twas full of dread,
  of smoke and fiery breath,
And no man dare put foot in there
  for fear of pain and death.

"But I was made all unafraid,
  so, careless and alone,
Day after day I made my way
  into that land unknown;
Night after night by camp-fire light
  I crouched in lonely thought;
Oh, gentle youth, this is the truth—
  I knew not what I sought.

"I rose at dawn; I wandered on.
  'Tis somewhat fine and grand

To be alone and hold your own
        in God's vast awesome land;
Come woe or weal, 'tis fine to feel
        a hundred miles between
    The trails you dare and pathways where
        the feet of men have been.

"And so it fell on me a spell
        of wander-lust was cast.
    The land was still and strange and chill,
        and cavernous and vast;
And sad and dead, and dull as lead,
        the valleys sought the snows;
    And far and wide on every side
        the ashen peaks arose.

"The moon was like a silent spike
        that pierced the sky right through;
    The small stars popped and winked and hopped
        in vastitudes of blue;
And unto me for company
        came creatures of the shade,
    And formed in rings and whispered things
        that made me half afraid.

"And strange though be, 'twas borne on me
        that land had lived of old,
    And men had crept and slain and slept
        where now they toiled for gold;
Through jungles dim the mammoth grim
        had sought the oozy fen,
    And on his track, all bent of back,
        had crawled the hairy men.

"And furthermore, strange deeds of yore
    in this dead place were done.
They haunted me, as wild and free
    I roamed from sun to sun;
Until I came where sudden flame
    uplit a terraced height,
    A regnant peak that seemed to seek
        the coronal of night.

"I scaled the peak; my heart was weak,
    yet on and on I pressed.
Skyward I strained until I gained
    its dazzling silver crest;
And there I found, with all around
    a world supine and stark,
    Swept clean of snow, a flat plateau,
        and on it lay—the Ark.

"Yes, there, I knew, by two and two
    the beasts did disembark,
And so in haste I ran and traced
    in letters on the Ark
My human name—Ben Smith's the same.
    And now I want to float
    A syndicate to haul and freight
        to town that noble boat."

I met him later in a bar and made a gay remark
Anent on ancient miner and an option on the Ark.
He gazed at me reproachfully, as only topers can;
But what he said I can't repeat—he was a bad old man.

31

The Low-Down White

This is the pay-day up at the mines,
    when the bearded brutes come down
  There's money to burn in the streets to-night,
    so I've sent my klooch to town,
With a haggard face and a ribband of red
    entwined in her hair of brown.

And I know at the dawn she'll come reeling home
    with the bottles, one, two, three—
  One for herself, to drown her shame,
    and two big bottles for me,
To make me forget the thing I am
    and the man I used to be.

To make me forget the brand of the dog,
    as I crouch in this hideous place;
  To make me forget once I kindled the light
    of love in a lady's face,
Where even the squalid Siwash now
    holds me a black disgrace.

Oh, I have guarded my secret well!
    And who would dream as I speak
In a tribal tongue like a rogue unhung,
    'mid the ranchhouse filth and reek,
I could roll to bed with a Latin phrase
    and rise with a verse of Greek?

Yet I was a senior prizeman once,
    and the pride of a college eight;
Called to the bar—my friends were true!
    but they could not keep me straight;
Then came the divorce, and I went abroad
    and "died" on the River Plate.

But I'm not dead yet; though with half a lung,
    there isn't time to spare,
And I hope that the year will see me out,
    and, thank God, no one will care—
Save maybe the little slim Siwash girl
    with the rose of shame in her hair.

She will come with the dawn, and the dawn is near;
    I can see its evil glow,
Like a corpse-light seen through a frosty pane
    in a night of want and woe;
And yonder she comes by the bleak bull-pines,
    swift staggering through the snow.

The Man from Eldorado

He's the man from Eldorado,
    and he's just arrived in town,
  In moccasins and oily buckskin shirt.
He's gaunt as any Indian, and pretty nigh as brown;
    He's greasy, and he smells of sweat and dirt.
He sports a crop of whiskers that would shame a healthy hog;
    Hard work has racked his joints and stooped his back;
He slops along the sidewalk followed by his yellow dog,
    But he's got a bunch of gold-dust in his sack.

He seems a little wistful as he blinks at all the lights,
    And maybe he is thinking of his claim
And the dark and dwarfish cabin
    where he lay and dreamed at nights,
    (Thank God, he'll never see the place again!)
Where he lived on tinned tomatoes,
    beef embalmed and sourdough bread,
  On rusty beans and bacon furred with mold;
His stomach's out of kilter and his system full of lead,
    But it's over, and his poke is full of gold.

He has panted at the windlass, he has loaded in the drift,
    He has pounded at the face of oozy clay;
He has taxed himself to sickness,

dark and damp and double shift,
　　He has labored like a demon night and day.
And now, praise God, it's over, and he seems to breathe again
　　Of new-mown hay, the warm, wet, friendly loam;
He sees a snowy orchard in a green and dimpling plain,
　　And a little vine-clad cottage, and it's—Home.

II.

He's the man from Eldorado,
　　and he's had a bite and sup,
　　And he's met in with a drouthy friend or two;
He's cached away his gold-dust, but he's sort of bucking up,
　　So he's kept enough tonight to see him through.
His eye is bright and genial, his tongue no longer lags;
　　His heart is brimming o'er with joy and mirth;
He may be far from savory, he may be clad in rags,
　　But to-night he feels as if he owns the earth.

Says he, "Boys, here is where the shaggy
　　North and I will shake;
　　I thought I'd never manage to get free.
I kept on making misses; but at last I've got my stake;
　　There's no more thawing frozen muck for me.
I am going to God's Country, where I'll live the simple life;
　　I'll buy a bit of land and make a start;
I'll carve a little homestead, and I'll win a little wife,
　　And raise ten little kids to cheer my heart."

They signified their sympathy by crowding to the bar;
　　They bellied up three deep and drank his health.
He shed a radiant smile around and smoked a rank cigar;
　　They wished him honor, happiness, and wealth.
They drank unto his wife to be—that unsuspecting maid;

They drank unto his children half a score;
And when they got through drinking, very tenderly they laid
    The man from Eldorado on the floor.

III.

He's the man from Eldorado,
        and he's only starting in
    To cultivate a thousand-dollar jag.
His poke is full of gold-dust and his heart is full of sin,
    And he's dancing with a girl called Muckluck Mag.
She's as light as any fairy; she's as pretty as a peach;
    She's mistress of the witchcraft to beguile;
There's sunshine in her manner, there is music in her speech,
    And there's concentrated honey in her smile.

Oh, the fever of the dance-hall and the glitter and the shine,
    The beauty, and the jewels, and the whirl,
The madness of the music, the rapture of the wine,
    The languorous allurement of a girl!

She is like a lost madonna; he is gaunt, unkempt and grim;
　　But she fondles him and gazes in his eyes;
Her kisses seek his heavy lips, and soon it seems to him
　　He has staked a little claim in Paradise.

"Who's for a juicy two-step?" cries the master of the floor;
　　The music throbs with soft, seductive beat.
There's glitter, gilt and gladness; there are pretty girls galore;
　　There's a woolly man with moccasins on feet.
They know they've got him going; he is buying wine for all;
　　They crowd around as buzzards at a feast,
Then when his poke is empty, they boost him from the hall,
　　And spurn him in the gutter like a beast.

He's the man from Eldorado,
　　　　and he's painting red the town;
　　Behind he leaves a trail of yellow dust;
In a whirl of senseless riot he is ramping up and down;
　　There's nothing checks his madness and his lust.
And soon the word is passed around—it travels like a flame;
　　They fight to clutch his hand and call him friend,
The chevaliers of lost repute, the dames of sorry fame;
　　Then comes the grim awakening—the end.

IV.

He's the man from Eldorado,
　　　　and he gives a grand affair;
　　There's feasting, dancing, wine without restraint.
The smooth Beau Brummels of the bar, the faro men, are there;
　　The tinhorns and purveyors of red paint;
The sleek and painted women, their predacious eyes aglow—
　　Sure Klondike City never saw the like;

Then Muckluck Mag proposed the toast: "The giver of the show,
   The livest sport that ever hit the pike."

The "live one" rises to his feet; he stammers to reply—
   And then there comes before his muddled brain
A vision of green vastitudes beneath an April sky,
   And clover pastures drenched with silver rain.
He knows that it can never be, that he is down and out;
   Life leers at him with foul and fetid breath;
And then amid the revelry, the song and cheer and shout,
   He suddenly grows grim and cold as death.

He grips the table tensely, and he says, "Dear friends of mine,
   I've let you dip your fingers in my purse;
I've crammed you at my table,
      and I've drowned you in my wine,
   And I've little left to give you but—my curse.
I've failed supremely in my plans; it's rather late to whine;
   My poke is mighty weasened up and small.
I thank you each for coming here; the happiness is mine—
   And now, you thieves and harlots, take it all."

V.

He twists the thong from off his poke; he swings it o'er his head;
   The nuggets fall around their feet like grain.
They rattle over roof and wall; they scatter, roll and spread;
   The dust is like a shower of golden rain.
The guests a moment stand aghast, then grovel on the floor;
   They fight, and snarl, and claw, like beasts of prey;
And then, as everybody gabbed and everybody swore,
   The man from Eldorado slipped away.

He's the man from Eldorado,
     and they found him stiff and dead,
    Half covered by the freezing ooze and dirt.
A clotted Colt was in his hand, a hole was in his head,
    And he wore an old and oily buckskin shirt.
His eyes were fixed and horrible, as one who hails the end;
    The frost had set him rigid as a log;
And there, half lying on his breast, his last and only friend,
    There crouched and whined a mangy yellow dog.

The Harpy

There was a woman, and she was wise; woefully wise was she;
She was old, so old, yet her years all told were but a score and three;
And she knew by heart, from finish to start, the Book of Iniquity.

There is no hope for such as I
        on earth, nor yet in Heaven;
Unloved I live, unloved I die,
        unpitied, unforgiven;
A loathed jade, I ply my trade,
        unhallowed and unshriven.

I paint my cheeks, for they are white,
        and cheeks of chalk men hate;
Mine eyes with wine I make to shine,
        that man may seek and sate;
With overhead a lamp of red
        I sit me down and wait

Until they come, the nightly scum,
        with drunken eyes aflame;
Your sweethearts, sons, ye scornful ones—
        'tis I who know their shame.
The gods, ye see, are brutes to me—
        and so I play my game.

For life is not the thing we thought,
    and not the thing we plan;
  And Woman in a bitter world
    must do the best she can—
Must yield the stroke, and bear the yoke,
    and serve the will of man;

Must serve his need and ever feed
    the flame of his desire,
  Though be she loved for love alone,
    or be she loved for hire;
For every man since life began
    is tainted with the mire.

And though you know he love you so
    and set you on love's throne;
Yet let your eyes but mock his sighs,
    and let your heart be stone,
Lest you be left (as I was left)
    attainted and alone.

From love's close kiss to hell's abyss
    is one sheer flight, I trow,
  And wedding ring and bridal bell
    are will-o'-wisps of woe,
And 'tis not wise to love too well,
    and this all women know.

Wherefore, the wolf-pack having gorged
    upon the lamb, their prey,
  With siren smile and serpent guile
    I make the wolf-pack pay—
With velvet paws and flensing claws,
    a tigress roused to slay.

One who in youth sought truest truth
    and found a devil's lies;
  A symbol of the sin of man,
    a human sacrifice.
Yet shall I blame on man the shame?
    Could it be otherwise?

Was I not born to walk in scorn
    where others walk in pride?
  The Maker marred, and, evil-starred,
    I drift upon His tide;
And He alone shall judge His own,
    so I His judgment bide.

Fate has written a tragedy; its name is "The Human Heart."
  The Theatre is the House of Life, Woman the mummer's part;
The Devil enters the prompter's box, and the play is ready to start.

The Ballad of One-Eyed Mike

This is the tale that was told to me
by the man with the crystal eye,
As I smoked my pipe in the campfire light,
and the Glories swept the sky;
As the Northlights gleamed and curved and streamed,
and the bottle of "hooch" was dry.

A man once aimed that my life be shamed,
and wrought me a deathly wrong;
I vowed one day I would well repay,
but the heft of his hate was strong.
He thonged me East and he thonged me West;
he harried me back and forth,
Till I fled in fright from his peerless spite
to the bleak, bald-headed North.

And there I lay, and for many a day
I hatched plan after plan,
For a golden haul of the wherewithal
to crush and to kill my man;
And there I strove, and there I clove
through the drift of icy streams;
And there I fought, and there I sought
for the pay-streak of my dreams.

So twenty years, with their hopes and fears
     and smiles and tears and such,
  Went by and left me long bereft
     of hope of the Midas touch;
About as fat as a chancel rat,
     and lo! despite my will,
  In the weary fight I had clean lost sight
     of the man I sought to kill.

'Twas so far away, that evil day
     when I prayed the Prince of Gloom
  For the savage strength and the sullen length
     of life to work his doom.
Nor sign nor word had I seen or heard,
     and it happed so long ago;
  My youth was gone and my memory wan,
     and I willed it even so.

It fell one night in the waning light
     by the Yukon's oily flow,
  I smoked and sat as I marvelled at
     the sky's port-winey glow;
Till it paled away to an absinthe gray,
     and the river seemed to shrink,
  All wobbly flakes and wriggling snakes
     and goblin eyes a-wink.

'Twas weird to see and it 'wildered me
     in a queer, hypnotic dream,
  Till I saw a spot like an inky blot
     come floating down the stream;
It bobbed and swung; it sheered and hung;
     it romped round in a ring;

It seemed to play in a tricksome way;
    it sure was a merry thing.

In freakish flights strange oily lights
    came fluttering round its head,
Like butterflies of a monster size—
    then I knew it for the Dead.
Its face was rubbed and slicked and scrubbed
    as smooth as a shaven pate;
In the silver snakes that the water makes
    it gleamed like a dinner-plate.

It gurgled near, and clear and clear
    and large and large it grew;
It stood upright in a ring of light
    and it looked me through and through.
It weltered round with a woozy sound,
    and ere I could retreat,
With the witless roll of a sodden soul
    it wantoned to my feet.

And here I swear by this Cross I wear,
    I heard that "floater" say:
"I am the man from whom you ran,
    the man you sought to slay.
That you may note and gaze and gloat,
    and say 'Revenge is sweet,'
In the grit and grime of the river's slime
    I am rotting at your feet.

"The ill we rue we must e'en undo,
    though it rive us bone from bone;
So it came about that I sought you out,

for I prayed I might atone.
I did you wrong, and for long and long
    I sought where you might live;
      And now you're found, though I'm dead and drowned,
        I beg you to forgive."

So sad it seemed, and its cheek-bones gleamed,
     and its fingers flicked the shore;
    And it lapped and lay in a weary way,
      and its hands met to implore;
That I gently said: "Poor, restless dead,
    I would never work you woe;
      Though the wrong you rue you can ne'er undo,
        I forgave you long ago."

Then, wonder-wise, I rubbed my eyes
    and I woke from a horrid dream.
    The moon rode high in the naked sky,
      and something bobbed in the stream.
It held my sight in a patch of light,
     and then it sheered from the shore;
    It dipped and sank by a hollow bank,
      and I never saw it more.

This was the tale he told to me,
    that man so warped and gray,
    Ere he slept and dreamed, and the camp-fire gleamed
      in his eye in a wolfish way—
That crystal eye that raked the sky
    in the weird Auroral ray.

The Law of the Yukon

This is the law of the Yukon,
    and ever she makes it plain:
   "Send not your foolish and feeble;
    send me your strong and your sane—
Strong for the red rage of battle;
    sane, for I harry them sore;
   Send me men girt for the combat,
    men who are grit to the core;
Swift as the panther in triumph,
    fierce as the bear in defeat,
   Sired of a bulldog parent,
    steeled in the furnace heat.

"Send me the best of your breeding,
    lend me your chosen ones;
   Them will I take to my bosom,
    them will I call my sons;
Them will I gild with my treasure,
    them will I glut with my meat;
   But the others—the misfits, the failures—
    I trample them under my feet.
Dissolute, damned and despairful,
    crippled and palsied and slain,

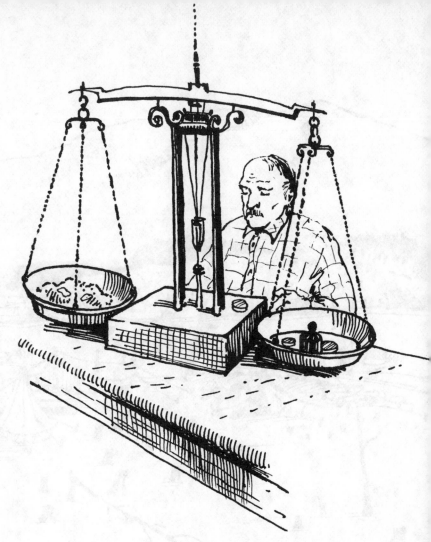

Ye would send me the spawn of your gutters—
    Go! take back your spawn again!

"Wild and wide are my borders,
        stern as death is my sway;
From my ruthless throne I have ruled alone
        for a million years and a day;
Hugging my mighty treasure,
        waiting for man to come,

Till he swept like a turbid torrent,
    and after him swept—the scum.
The pallid pimp of the dead-line,
    the enervate of the pen,
One by one I weeded them out,
    for all that I sought was—Men.

"One by one I dismayed them,
    frighting them sore with my glooms;
One by one I betrayed them
    unto my manifold dooms.
Drowned them like rats on my rivers,
    starved them like curs on my plains,
Rotted the flesh that was left them,
    poisoned the blood in their veins;
Burst with my winter upon them,
    searing forever their sight,
Lashed them with fungus-white faces,
    whimpering wild in the night;

"Staggering blind through the storm-whirl,
    stumbling mad through the snow,
Frozen stiff in the ice-pack,
    brittle and bent like a bow;
Featureless, formless, forsaken,
    scented by wolves in their flight,
Left for the wind to make music,
    through ribs that are glittering white;
Gnawing the black crust of failure,
    searching the pit of despair,
Crooking the toe in the trigger,
    trying to patter a prayer;

"Going outside with an escort,
        raving with lips all afoam,
Writing a check for a million,
        driveling feebly of home;
Lost like a louse in the burning...
        or else in the tented town
Seeking a drunkard's solace,
        sinking and sinking down;
Steeped in the slime at the bottom,
        dead to a decent world,
Lost 'mid the human flotsam,
        far on the frontier hurled;

"In the camp at the bend of the river,
        with its dozen saloons aglare,
Its gambling dens ariot,
        its gramophones all ablare;
Crimped with the crimes of a city,
        sin-ridden and bridled with lies,
In the hush of my mountained vastness,
        in the flush of my midnight skies.
Plague-spots, yet tools of my purpose,
        so natheless I suffer them thrive,
Crushing my Weak in their clutches,
        that only my Strong may survive.

"But the others, the men of my mettle,
        the men who would 'stablish my fame
Unto its ultimate issue,
        winning me honor, not shame;
Searching my uttermost valleys,
        fighting each step as they go.
Shooting the wrath of my rapids,

scaling my ramparts of snow;
Ripping the guts of my mountains,
    looting the beds of my creeks,
Them will I take to my bosom,
    and speak as a mother speaks.

"I am the land that listens,
    I am the land that broods;
Steeped in eternal beauty,
    crystalline waters and woods.
Long have I waited lonely,
    shunned as a thing accurst,
Monstrous, moody, pathetic,
    the last of the lands and the first;
Visioning campfires at twilight,
    sad with a longing forlorn,
Feeling my womb o'er-pregnant
    with the seeds of cities unborn.

"Wild and wide are my borders,
    stern as death is my sway,
And I wait for the men who will win me—
    and I will not be won in a day;
And I will not be won by weaklings,
    subtle, suave and mild,
But by men with the hearts of Vikings,
    and the simple faith of a child;
Desperate, strong and resistless,
    unthrottled by fear or defeat,
Them will I gild with my treasure,
    Them will I glut with my meat.

"Loftly I stand from each sister land,
  patient and wearily wise,
With the weight of a world of sadness
  in my quiet, passionless eyes;
Dreaming alone of a people,
  dreaming alone of a day,
When men shall not rape my riches,
  and curse me and go away;
Making a bawd of my bounty,
  fouling the hand that gave—
Till I rise in my wrath and I sweep on their path
  and I stamp them into a grave;

"Dreaming of men who will bless me,
  of women esteeming me good,
Of children born in my borders
  of radiant motherhood,
Of cities leaping to stature,
  of fame like a flag unfurled,
As I pour the tide of my riches
  in the eager lap of the world."

This is the law of the Yukon,
  that only the Strong shall thrive;
That surely the Weak shall perish,
  and only the Fit survive.
Dissolute, damned and despairful,
  crippled and palsied and slain,
This is the Will of the Yukon—
  Lo, how she makes it plain!